WOLFGRAN RETURNS!

Finbar O'Connor is a graduate of Trinity College and King's Inns, Dublin. Having spent years working as a librarian in his native Drumcondra, he is now a practising barrister. He is the author of *Wolfgran*, the prequel to *Wolfgran Returns*! He has also published songs, stories and poetry. He lives in Drumcondra with his wife and two daughters.

Martin Fagan is an illustrator and cartoonist.

For Aidan Levey

Finbar O'Connor
Illustrated by Martin Fagan

THE O'BRIEN PRESS
DUBLIN

First published 2004 by The O'Brien Press Ltd,
20 Victoria Road, Dublin 6, Ireland.
Tel: +353 1 4923333; Fax: +353 1 4922777
E-mail: books@obrien.ie
Website: www.obrien.ie

ISBN: 0-86278-884-6

British Library Cataloguing-in-Publication Data
A catalogue record for this title is available from the British Library

1 2 3 4 5 6
04 05 06 07 08

The O'Brien Press receives
assistance from

Editing, typesetting, layout, design: The O'Brien Press Ltd
Printing: Cox & Wyman

Contents

Chapter One

Crime Wave

Ever since the day the Big Bad Wolf had come into the city disguised as Little Red Riding Hood's Grandmother and swallowed most of the police force, Chief Inspector Plonker had been determined to catch him. He even went on television to warn the citizens of the city that a Wolf disguised as an old lady was prowling the streets swallowing people. He called this fiendish creature The Wolfgran. A big reward was offered to anybody who captured it. Unfortunately, some people tried to claim the reward by grabbing any old ladies who happened to be passing and dragging them into the nearest police station. Soon every cell in the city had an old lady locked up in it, and the police were running out of tea and digestive biscuits. Of course, none of these prisoners was the Wolfgran. In the end the offer of a reward had to be withdrawn, and the old ladies were released.

Then the city was hit by a terrible crime wave. An old lady rushed into the post office, snarled at the postmistress and stole all the stamps. Another old lady went into the supermarket, filled her trolley with cat food and tea bags, threatened to swallow the checkout girl and ran out without paying! But when nine different old ladies on the

BUS

same bus all claimed to be the Wolfgran and refused to pay their bus fares, Inspector Plonker realised what was happening. Knowing that everybody was terrified of the Wolfgran, little old ladies were turning to crime!

One morning the Chief of Police barged into Inspector Plonker's office and started shouting at him.

'You've got to do something about this Wolfgran business, Plonker,' he yelled, 'Somebody's grandmother just mugged me and nicked my wallet!'

'Was it the Wolfgran, sir?' asked Inspector Plonker.

'How should I know?' yelled the Chief of Police. 'But I wasn't taking any chances. These old biddies are taking over the city! Did you know they've started refusing to pay their library fines? Even that old dragon the

City Librarian is scared of them now!'

'But what can I do, Chief?' asked the Inspector, 'We can't lock them all up. We haven't got the cell space, not to mention the toilet facilities!'

'You don't have to lock them all up, Plonker,' said the Chief of Police, 'You just have to catch the Wolfgran. Once he's under lock and key these old fossils will have to stop pretending to be wolves in disguise. Their reign of terror will be over and we'll have some law and order around here again!'

'I'll do my best, Chief,' said Inspector Plonker.

'You'll need to do better that that, Plonker,' said the Chief, 'I'm giving you twenty-four hours to get the Wolfgran off the streets. Otherwise you're off the force!'

When the Chief had left, Inspector

Plonker pressed the buzzer on his telephone that summoned his assistant, Sergeant Snoop. The Inspector was hoping the Sergeant might have some bright ideas. But when his office door opened it was not Sergeant Snoop who entered, but the Big Bad Wolf himself! He wasn't even in his usual disguise as an old lady, and the glowing eyes, enormous teeth and long, shaggy tail were unmistakable.

Inspector Plonker leaped to his feet, drew his gun and pointed it at the intruder.

'Police! Freeze!' he barked. 'You're under arrest!'

But the Wolf only grinned at him. Then, to the Inspector's horror, he heard the voice of Sergeant Snoop, which seemed to be coming from the belly of the beast!

'Sorry, sir,' said Sergeant Snoop, 'We didn't mean to startle you!'

'Good grief, Snoop!' cried the Inspector, 'Is that you in there?'

'It certainly is, sir,' replied Sergeant Snoop, 'And Constable Perkins is in here with me. We were hoping you might be able to get us out.'

'You fiend!' snarled Inspector Plonker, glaring at the Wolf. 'How dare you swallow my sergeant!'

The Wolf said nothing, but just went right on grinning.

'Think it's funny, do you?' barked the Inspector. 'Well, you'll smirk on the other side of your face when I blow your head off!'

'Don't shoot, sir,' cried sergeant Snoop, 'It's not the wolf. It's just a costume!'

'What are you talking about, Snoop?'

asked the Inspector, still pointing his gun at the wolf's head.

'It's for the annual station pantomime, sir,' said Sergeant Snoop, 'We're doing "The Three Little Pigs" this year. Perkins and I are playing the Wolf. Perkins made the costume himself!'

'But you said you'd been swallowed, Snoop,' said the Inspector, lowering his gun. 'You said you wanted me to get you out!'

'I meant get us out of the costume, sir,' replied sergeant Snoop. 'The zip is stuck, you see!'

'I knew I should've used buttons,' said the voice of Constable Perkins.

But Inspector Plonker was looking thoughtful.

'Tell me, Snoop,' he said, as he holstered his gun and opened the zip that ran down the front of the costume, 'When is the first performance?'

'Tonight, sir,' said Sergeant Snoop as he struggled out of the wolf suit, followed by Constable Perkins. 'We just had our final dress rehearsal!'

'Well, cancel it, Snoop,' barked Inspector Plonker.

'Cancel the show?' gasped Constable Perkins. 'We can't do that!'

'You'll have to,' said Inspector Plonker. 'I'm commandeering that wolf suit. Important Police business!'

'But what about the show, sir?' asked Sergeant Snoop. 'What shall we tell the rest of the cast? What shall we tell the public? My Mum bought six tickets!'

Inspector Plonker drew himself up to his full height and a steely glint came into his eyes.

'Tell them the safety of the city is at stake, Snoop,' he said grimly. 'And the safety of the city is more important than show business!'

Chapter Two

Tea Cosies and Cardigans

Meanwhile, in his secret den deep in the forest, the real Wolf was looking gloomily at his reflection in the mirror.

His nightdress was definitely looking a bit shabby, and his sharp claws were poking out through the tops of his pink, fluffy slippers. As for his handbag, the strap was broken and the lining was torn. This was because, while most old ladies use their handbags to carry purses, pension books and peppermints, the Wolf used his for whacking squirrels.

He also found it very useful for clobbering ducks and stunning pigeons. You see, one great thing about being a wolf disguised as a little old lady is this: If you sit on a park bench for long enough, pretending to eat a sandwich, sooner or later you will be approached by a duck, a squirrel or a pigeon, hoping to scrounge a few crumbs. Then you simply whack them with your handbag, stuff them into it, close it with a click and wait for your next victim.

This was how the Wolf caught his dinner every day. As a result, the ducks in the park had become very nervous of old ladies, the pigeons pooped on their hats and the squirrels kept throwing acorns at them.

But there was another reason why the Wolf spent all his time disguised as an old lady: The forest had become far too dangerous. Everybody was out to get him. The three pigs had got so fed up with his huffing and puffing and blowing their house down that they had bought a big pack of ferocious wolfhounds, which they set on him every time he came near their property.

As for Granny Riding Hood, she had brought her nephew Horace the woodcutter to live with her. The last time the wolf had crept up to her cottage and lisped, 'Gwanny, it is I, Wittle Wed Widing Hood,' a big, hairy man wearing a check shirt had almost chopped his head off with an axe!

So the Wolf decided that it was probably safer to stay in disguise. But the problem was his clothes were beginning to wear out. More and more shaggy fur was showing through the various rips, tears and holes in his nightdress. It was only a matter of time before somebody saw through his disguise.

This was why, as he examined his reflection, the Wolf was looking so gloomy. He had realised that there was only one thing for it. He would have to sneak into Granny Riding Hood's cottage and steal a new outfit. He would do it that very evening, as he had spotted a perfect opportunity for this dangerous mission. On his way to the park that day he had seen a big sign outside the Town Hall. It said:

Massive Bingo Gala Night
Fabulous Prizes
Tea Cosies
Slippers
Cat Food
Cardigans
Tonight, eight o'clock sharp

The Wolf knew that Granny Riding Hood loved bingo and could never resist the chance to win a tea cosy, so she was bound to go. His plan was to sneak into Granny's cottage while she was out, rummage through her wardrobe for a new outfit and be safely gone before she got back. In his new disguise, he would be safe from woodcutters and wolfhounds.

So, later that evening the Wolf made his way to Granny Riding Hood's cottage. He hid behind a tree and waited for her to leave. He had already seen Horace chopping down trees in another part of the forest, so he knew she was alone. Before long Granny came out the back door and hurried off down the garden path.

Now, the wolf was so excited about getting a new disguise that instead of waiting to check that Granny had actually gone off to bingo, he simply slipped in the front door and started rooting through her wardrobe. That was why he did not see her going into the little outhouse at the bottom of the garden that was actually her outdoor lavatory. Once inside the house, the Wolf sat down in granny's rocking chair and began trying on different pairs of pink fluffy slippers.

A few minutes later Inspector Plonker and Sergeant Snoop, dressed in the pantomime wolf costume, came shuffling through the trees towards the cottage.

'Now remember, Snoop,' said Inspector Plonker, 'I'll do all the talking!'

'But you're the back end, sir!' objected Sergeant Snoop.

'So what?' asked the Inspector.

'Well, sir,' said Sergeant Snoop, 'Aren't people going to think you're talking through your ...?'

'Don't be impertinent, Snoop,' snapped Inspector Plonker.

'Anyway, sir,' continued Sergeant Snoop, 'I still don't see why we have to be in disguise to catch the Wolf.'

'I've explained this to you before, Snoop,' said Inspector Plonker. 'It's standard police procedure. It's called working undercover. If you want to catch a crook you pretend to be a crook yourself. Then you make friends with him, join his gang and, just as he's about to commit a crime, you nab him!'

'I see, sir,' said Sergeant Snoop. 'So we're going to pretend to be a wolf, make friends with the real Wolf, wait until he tries to swallow somebody, then nab him?'

'Precisely, Snoop,' said Inspector Plonker. 'It's how they always catch criminals on TV.'

'But you've never actually caught a criminal, sir,' said Sergeant Snoop.

'Nonsense, Snoop,' said Inspector Plonker. 'What about the Bearded Burglar?'

'The who?' asked Sergeant Snoop.

'Oh, you were on your holidays at the time, Snoop,' said Inspector Plonker. 'Christmas Eve I think it was. I spotted this old chap sneaking down people's chimneys with a big sack, so I nabbed him and threw him in the cells.'

'This old chap,' said Sergeant Snoop, 'He had a beard, did he?'

'Of course he did, Snoop,' said Inspector Plonker. 'That's why I call him the Bearded Burglar!'

‘He wasn’t dressed in red, was he, sir?’ asked Sergeant Snoop.

‘He was as a matter of fact,’ replied Inspector Plonker, ‘and he had the most horrible laugh I’ve ever heard in my life! Why, I can almost hear it now!’

‘“Ho! Ho! Ho!” sir?’ asked Sergeant Snoop.

‘That’s it exactly, Snoop!’ exclaimed the Inspector. ‘You’ve heard of him then, have you? Notorious criminal I suppose?’

‘He’s quite famous all right, sir,’ said Sergeant Snoop. ‘Tell me, sir, what was in the sack?’

‘Toys, Snoop,’ said Inspector Plonker, ‘and when I nicked him he said I’d have to let him go ’cos he hadn’t done the orphanage yet! I mean, I’ve met some fiends in my time, but to go around stealing toys from orphans, and at Christmas too!'

'Have you ever heard of Santa Claus, sir?' asked Sergeant Snoop.

'Who?' asked the Inspector.

'Don't you realise that none of the children in the city got any presents last year, sir?' asked Sergeant Snoop.

'Of course they didn't, Snoop,' said Inspector Plonker. 'The Bearded Burglar nicked the lot! But next year will be different!'

'Why is that, sir?' asked Sergeant Snoop.

'I told him next time I caught him I'd throw the book at him,' said Inspector Plonker triumphantly. 'He won't be showing his face around here again in a hurry!'

'Inspector Plonker,' said Sergeant Snoop, finally losing patience, 'you are a complete and utter ...'

'Genius, Snoop?' said Inspector Plonker. 'Don't worry, my lad. Learn from me, observe my methods and some day you too can be a great detective! Now, let's take a look in this cottage. For all we know the Wolf may be lurking there already!'

Chapter Three

Thick as a Turnip

The Wolf was in the cottage all right, but he wasn't doing any lurking. In fact, at the moment he heard the knock on the door, he was busily trying on cardigans. Licking his lips at the thought that it might be Little Red Riding Hood (but also a bit nervous in case it was Horace and his hatchet), he opened the door an inch or so and peered through the crack. When he saw another wolf standing on the doorstep he was absolutely furious.

'Beggar off!' he roared. 'Go and eat some other old woman.'

'Don't worry, Granny Riding Hood,' said Inspector Plonker, 'we are undercover policemen. We have reason to believe the Big Bad Wolf often frequents this cottage. Have you seen him lately?'

'Who, me?' exclaimed the Wolf, realising that the Inspector did not see through his disguise, 'Er … no.'

'Perhaps a description would help,' said the Inspector. 'Carry on, Sergeant!'

'Sir!' said Sergeant Snoop, producing his notebook and reading aloud, 'The Wolf has red glowing eyes …'

'Horrible!' exclaimed the Wolf, putting on a pair of sunglasses to hide his eyes.

'… big furry ears …' continued Sergeant Snoop.

'Dreadful!' exclaimed the Wolf, putting on a hat to hide his ears.

'... a long, shaggy tail ...' read Sergeant Snoop.

'Whoops!' exclaimed the Wolf, stuffing his tail into his pocket.

' ... and sharp, pointy teeth.' droned Sergeant Snoop.

'Mmmmph!' said the Wolf, closing his mouth to hide his teeth.

'So if you see anybody around who looks like that, be sure to let us know,' said Inspector Plonker, who was looking out the window.

'Oh, mmmph! Mmmph!' said the Wolf, nodding vigorously.

'Good grief, it's him!' yelled Inspector Plonker suddenly.

'Yikes!' yelped the Wolf, thinking he'd been recognised.

'Where, sir?' asked Sergeant Snoop.

'Out there, look!' cried Inspector Plonker, and he pointed out the window to where Granny Riding Hood was coming up the garden path.

'The fiend,' said Inspector Plonker. 'He's disguised as an old lady again.'

'Tsh! Tsk! Tsk!' said the Wolf, shaking his head disapprovingly.

'Mind you, he doesn't fool me for a second,' said the Inspector. 'I mean, only a complete idiot would be taken in by that disguise.'

'Complete idiot,' said the Wolf, nodding vigorously.

'You'd want to be as thick as a turnip not to be able to tell a little old lady from a wolf anyway,' chortled the Inspector.

'Thick as a turnip,' repeated the Wolf, nodding even more vigorously.

'What'll we do, sir?' asked Sergeant Snoop, 'He's nearly at the door.'

'Well,' said Inspector Plonker, 'if Granny here hides in the wardrobe and starts banging on the door and yelling, we'll tell the wolf we've got Little Red Riding Hood trapped in there. Then, when he goes to have a look, we'll grab him and slap on the handcuffs. Think you can pretend to be Red Riding Hood, Granny?'

'No problem,' said the Wolf, who was very good at imitating Little Red Riding Hood's voice. After all, he'd had lots of practice.

Then he nipped into the wardrobe, shut the door behind him and crouched in the darkness, chuckling and muttering, 'Thick as an idiot,' and, 'A complete turnip,' over and over again.

Chapter Four

Who's Who?

The reason Granny had spent so long in the lavatory is that she had been reading a murder mystery called The Case of the Bloody Bones, which she had just borrowed from the library. (All old ladies love this kind of book. The next time you are in the library, just watch what they are taking out. The sweeter and kindlier an old lady looks, the more likely she is to borrow books with titles like The Mystery of the Slaughtered Sleuth or The Adventure of the Throttled Thrush.)

Important notice from the publishers:

We are sorry to interrupt, but we have just received a letter from an old lady who is very annoyed about the last paragraph and we thought we should bring it to your attention immediately:

Dear Sir or Madam,

I have just finished reading the last paragraph and I am very annoyed about it. I am an old lady and I do not read murder mysteries. I only read nice books about embroidery and flower arranging. It is disgraceful to allow this so-called author to imply that old ladies such as myself ever think of violence or mayhem. We are too busy baking and plumping up cushions.

Yours crankily,
An Old Lady

PS. Tell him if he doesn't stop writing this sort of thing about old ladies we will come around to his house and dodder at him!

Anyway, Granny had been so absorbed by her book that she had not noticed how late it was getting. Now she was in a hurry to catch the bus for the big bingo game. She hurried up the garden path, pushed open the back door and froze. There was a large wolf standing

in her living room. It was a peculiar-looking creature. Its shaggy pelt looked moth-eaten and it had what looked like a zipper running down its front, but the glowing eyes and slavering jaws looked wolfish enough.

As soon as Granny came into the cottage, the real Wolf, who was watching through a crack in the wardrobe door, began yelling and screaming, 'Save me, Granny, save me! It is I, Little Red Riding Hood. The wicked wolf has locked me in the wardrobe.'

Now, you might expect an old lady who comes back from the bathroom and finds that a wolf has locked her granddaughter in the wardrobe to scream and faint, or perhaps make a run (or at least a hobble) for it. But Granny Riding Hood was used to wolves. In fact she half-expected to find one lurking in her cottage from time to time, and had taken steps to deal with the problem. So, instead of screaming, fainting, running or hobbling, she merely opened the back door and yelled: 'Horace! He's back again!'

'Coming, Auntie,' replied a deep voice. A moment later a gigantic hairy man carrying an enormous hatchet lumbered into the room. Horace was Granny Riding Hood's nephew. He was a woodcutter by trade and not very intelligent, but he knew how to deal with wolves.

'Shall I chop his head off, Auntie?' asked Horace, raising his axe.

'Oh, I suppose so,' said Granny irritably, 'though he'll make a right mess of the carpet.'

'I could just wring his neck,' suggested Horace.

'Oh, could you?' asked Granny gratefully. 'Only I just washed that rug this morning.'

'Right, Auntie,' said Horace, putting down his axe and cracking his knuckles.

'Now, just a minute,' said Inspector Plonker as Horace advanced towards him, 'I am Chief Inspector Plonker of the City Police.'

Horace paused and stared at him.

'No, you're not,' he said. 'I've seen Inspector Plonker and he doesn't have ears like those.'

'And I'm Sergeant Snoop,' said Sergeant Snoop.

'I thought you were Inspector Plonker?' said Horace, puzzled.

'We're undercover,' said Inspector Plonker, 'This is a disguise.'

'Take it off then,' said Horace.

'Take it off, Snoop,' ordered Inspector Plonker.

'I can't, sir,' said Sergeant Snoop, 'The zip's stuck again.'

'A likely story,' scoffed Granny Riding Hood. 'Throttle him, Horace.'

'Right, Auntie,' said Horace, moving forward again.

'Just listen, will you?' yelled Inspector Plonker, 'It's not us you should be throttling, it's her, I mean him.'

'Who?' asked Horace, totally confused.

'Your Auntie!' yelled Inspector Plonker.

'You want me to throttle my Auntie?' asked Horace, horrified.

'She's not your Auntie,' said Inspector Plonker. 'She's the Wolf.'

'But you're the Wolf,' said Horace.

'You're the one with furry ears and a shaggy tail.'

'But mine aren't real,' yelled Inspector Plonker. 'His are.'

'Whose are?' asked Horace, looking more and more baffled.

'Your Auntie's,' yelled Inspector Plonker.

Horace looked closely at Granny Riding Hood's grey, curly hair. He couldn't see any furry ears, and it was obvious even to him that she didn't have a tail. He glared at Inspector Plonker.

'Stop talking through your bottom,' he said.

'Look, it's a wig, I'll show you,' cried Inspector Plonker. He reached out, grabbed Granny Riding Hood's hair and pulled vigorously.

'Ouch!' yelled granny Riding Hood. 'He's attacking me, Horace.'

‘Right, that’s it,’ said Horace, picking up his hatchet. ‘Nobody pulls my Auntie’s hair and gets away with it.’

‘But that’s not your Auntie, I tell you!’ cried Inspector Plonker as Horace raised the axe. ‘Your Auntie’s hiding in the wardrobe.’

‘He’s lying,’ yelled the Wolf from inside the wardrobe (where he had been sniggering happily at the Inspector’s dilemma). ‘I’m Little Red Riding Hood, I am.’

‘No, you’re not, you silly old bat,’ yelled Inspector Plonker.

‘Oh, just get on with it, Horace,’ said Granny Riding Hood. ‘I’m late for bingo.’

‘Right, Auntie,’ said Horace, lunging forward.

Inspector Plonker and Sergeant Snoop dodged him and dived through the window, shattering the glass and landing with a thump on the grass outside.

Granny watched until they had vanished into the trees, with Horace in hot pursuit. Then she went over to the wardrobe and opened the door.

'Out you come, dear,' she said, peering into the shadows. 'The Wolf is gone, you're quite safe now.'

In a trice the Wolf pounced, stuffed her into the wardrobe and locked it. He was heading for the front door when Granny's mobile phone, which she had left in her handbag on the table, began to ring.

Cautiously, the Wolf answered it.

'Hello?' he said.

'Granny?' said the voice of Little Red Riding Hood. 'Where are you? I've been waiting at this bus stop for ages.'

'I'm on my way, my dear,' quavered the Wolf, trying to sound like an old lady. 'I'm on my way.'

Chuckling wickedly to himself, the Wolf left the cottage and hurried off towards the bus stop where Little Red Riding Hood was waiting.

Chapter Five

A Good Hiding

It is not easy for two people wearing a pantomime wolf costume to climb a tall tree. However, it's surprising what you can do when you are being chased by an enraged woodcutter with a big hatchet who thinks you want to eat his Auntie. Inspector Plonker and Sergeant Snoop clung to the topmost branch of their tree and looked down nervously at the forest floor far below. After scratching his head and thinking for a moment, Horace began to chop down the tree.

Sergeant Snoop struggled to open the zip so that they could take the costume off. But it was no use. It was stuck fast.

'What are we going to do, sir?' asked Sergeant Snoop, as the tree began to creak and rock from side to side.

'Well, Snoop,' said Inspector Plonker, 'it looks to me like we are going to fall out of this tree and get our heads chopped off!'

But suddenly the tree began to sway wildly in a buffeting breeze and the two policemen were almost deafened by the rattling roar of a helicopter, which came swooping down and hovered right over their heads.

'Okay, Wolf,' yelled a familiar voice. 'Your ass is grass.'

'It's the Chief,' cried Inspector Plonker. 'We're saved, Snoop!'

It was indeed the Chief of Police, who had been patrolling the forest in the hope of spotting the Wolf. Now he could hardly believe his luck! He produced a double-barrelled shotgun and took careful aim.

'Don't shoot, Chief,' cried Inspector Plonker. 'Its me, Inspector Plonker.'

'No it's not,' replied the Chief. 'Plonker may not be very handsome, but even he doesn't have ears like yours.'

'Don't shoot, Chief,' yelled Sergeant Snoop. 'It's me, Sergeant Snoop.'

'You can't fool me, Wolf,' yelled the Chief. 'I know Sergeant Snoop, and he definitely doesn't have a long, shaggy tail.'

'Open that zip, Snoop,' bawled Inspector Plonker.

'I'm trying, sir, I'm trying,' screamed Sergeant Snoop.

'Your hide is fried, Wolf,' yelled the Chief of Police, slowly squeezing the trigger.

Desperately Sergeant Snoop reached up and grabbed one of the wheels of the helicopter.

'Hang on, sir,' he yelled and swung out of the tree. There was a deafening boom as the shotgun went off, blasting the branch the two policemen had been hanging onto a moment before.

'Trying to board me, eh?' sneered the Chief of Police, taking aim again as the helicopter sped over the forest with Sergeant Snoop and Inspector Plonker hanging on for dear life.

Now, one of the first things they teach you at helicopter school is that if you ever find a wolf dangling from your undercarriage you should not, under any circumstances, try to blast it with a shotgun. Of course, what the Chief of Police had dangling from his helicopter was not a wolf, but two policemen in a wolf suit. However, the same rule still applies. He definitely should not have started taking pot-shots at them.

Fortunately for Inspector Plonker and Sergeant Snoop, he missed them and shot off his tail rotor instead. The tail rotor is the small propeller at the back of the helicopter. Without it, instead of flying in a straight line, the helicopter spins round and round like a carousel. This is what the Chief's helicopter now began to do. As the Chief of Police struggled frantically with the controls, the stricken machine tumbled across the sky. Inspector Plonker and Sergeant Snoop watched as the forest passed in a green whirling blur below. Finally, as they reached the edge of the trees, the two policemen lost their grip and fell wailing towards the ground while the helicopter vanished into the distance.

Luckily for them, their fall was broken when they landed on the Wolf!

Not that the Wolf saw it that way of course. He had left the shelter of the forest and was nearly at the bus stop. He could see Little Red Riding Hood waving at him and shouting, 'Hello, Granny.' There was nobody else around, apart from a bunch of old ladies who were waiting for the bingo bus. The Wolf's plan was to grab Little Red Riding Hood and vanish back into the woods. He didn't think a few old ladies would cause him any problems.

And then the sky seemed to fall on his head.

Though in fact, as we know, it was not the sky – it was Sergeant Snoop and Inspector Plonker dressed as a pantomime wolf.

So, as I said, at first this seemed like a piece of luck, especially when Sergeant Snoop noticed that the old lady they had landed on had a long, shaggy tail!

'Sir,' he exclaimed, 'this old lady we just landed on has a long, shaggy tail!'

'Snoop,' groaned Inspector Plonker, 'I don't care if she has a cold, wet nose and soft, silky ears. Get me to a hospital.'

'But don't you understand, sir?' said Sergeant Snoop eagerly as the two policemen struggled to their feet. 'This must be the Wolfgran!'

'What?' exclaimed Inspector Plonker. 'Are you sure?'

'Yes, sir,' said Sergeant Snoop, 'it's a wolf dressed as an old lady. And there's Little Red Riding Hood over there. We've got him, sir.'

'Excellent,' said Inspector Plonker. 'I knew my plan would work. Slap the cuffs on him and we'll take him back to the station. I can't wait to see the expression on the Chief's face.'

But the Wolf was a quick thinker.

'Help, help!' he cried. 'I'm just a poor old woman being attacked by a wolf.'

'Help, help!' cried Little Red Riding Hood. 'The Big Bad Wolf is trying to eat my Granny.'

Inspector Plonker and Sergeant Snoop very quickly found themselves surrounded by a large crowd of very angry old ladies. They were muttering furiously and brandishing handbags, umbrellas and knitting needles.

'Attack a defenceless old woman, would you?' said one.

'Big hairy hooligan,' grumbled another.

'I blame the parents,' mumbled a third.

'Give him a good hiding,' quavered a fourth.

'Ladies, ladies,' said Inspector Plonker nervously, 'I assure you, we are police officers and we have just apprehended a dangerous criminal.'

'What did it say?' said the first old lady.

'Didn't hear a word of it,' said the second.

'Everybody mumbles nowadays,' said the third.

'Claims he's a policeman,' said a fourth.

'Not with those ears he ain't,' said a fifth.

‘Give him a good hiding,’ said the others.

As Sergeant Snoop desperately tried to unfasten the zip, the old ladies closed in and began whacking, prodding and poking the two cowering policemen.

Important notice from the publishers:

We interrupt this painful scene to bring you another letter from the same old lady who wrote before, who is even more upset about this paragraph than she was about the last one:

Dear Sir or Madam,

I am the same old lady who wrote before and I am even more upset about this paragraph than

I was about the last one. Old ladies do not beat up policemen at bus stops. They are far too busy watching afternoon quiz shows on the television and trying to remember where they left their false teeth. Old ladies are gentle and kind and wouldn't hurt a fly, so there.

Yours grumpily,

The Same Old Lady Who Wrote Before

PS. Tell this so-called author that if he does not stop writing nasty things about old ladies we will come around to his house and knock over his milk bottles.

When the bus arrived, the old ladies left Inspector Plonker and Sergeant Snoop lying in a heap on the pavement and climbed aboard, taking Little Red Riding Hood and the slightly dazed Wolf with them. The Wolf was delighted – he had fooled them into thinking that he was Granny Riding Hood and that the two policemen were the Big Bad Wolf. But he was also a little nervous. He had seen what they did to Inspector Plonker and Sergeant Snoop, and he was afraid that if he tried to snatch Little Red Riding Hood they would do the same to him!

On the other hand, now that they thought the Wolf was out of the way, they would never suspect he was actually on the bus with them. The Wolf grinned nastily. All he had to do was bide his time. His plan was working perfectly.

Chapter Six

Pet Patrol

If you have a television in your house then you may have watched a programme called 'Pet Patrol'. On this programme two vets called Bruce and Sheila drive around the city in a big green ambulance (which they call the Big Green Ambulance), rescuing animals that have been cruelly treated and finding them good homes with kind people. Bruce and Sheila are two big, strapping sun-tanned persons who always wear shorts, white socks and hiking boots.

Well, if you had been watching 'Pet Patrol' on the day that this story takes place, you would have seen the Big Green Ambulance parked beside a bus stop. Bruce was bent over something battered and hairy that was lying on the pavement, and Sheila was speaking earnestly into a microphone.

'G'day, viewers,' Sheila was saying, 'and welcome to "Pet Patrol". The Big Green Ambulance has been called to a bus stop just outside town where somebody seems to have been mistreating this poor old wolf. Bruce is just examining the little fella now. How's he doing, Bruce?'

'Not too good, Sheila, not too good,' replied Bruce. 'In fact, I think this is the worst case of cruelty to a wolf I've seen in a long time. It looks as though

somebody's been poking the poor little bloke with knitting needles!'

'Strewth, Bruce,' said Sheila. 'Why would anybody do that?'

'Oh, we get a lot of that at this time of year, Sheila,' said Bruce. 'People buy wolves as Christmas presents, then as soon as they get big and start eating the kids they just dump 'em on the street!'

'Blimey, Bruce, that's just awful,' said Sheila. 'Isn't there anything you can do for the poor little blighter?'

'Well, Sheila, he's pretty far gone,' said Bruce. 'I think the kindest thing we can do for him is to put him out of his misery.'

'Crikey, Bruce, that's really, really sad,' said Sheila. 'So what'll you do? Give the poor little beggar an injection?'

'Actually, Sheila,' said Bruce, 'I was thinking of just running him over with the Big Green Ambulance.'

'Fair dinkum, mate,' said Sheila, as Bruce climbed into the ambulance and started up the engine. 'Remember, viewers, a wolf is for life, not just for Christmas.'

Luckily, Sergeant Snoop and Inspector Plonker, who had been knocked unconscious by the old ladies, were starting to come around.

'Wait, wait,' cried Inspector Plonker. 'We're undercover police officers.'

'With those ears?' said Bruce scornfully. 'I don't think so, mate.'

'Right,' said Inspector Plonker, 'we're commandeering your vehicle.'

The two policemen sprang up, dragged Bruce out of the ambulance, jumped behind the wheel and drove off down the road towards the city.

'Well I'll be a dingo's do-dos, Bruce,' said Sheila. 'He's only gone and nicked the Big Green Ambulance!'

'The ungrateful brute,' exclaimed Bruce, 'And after all we've done for him.'

'Stay tuned, viewers,' said Sheila. 'We'll soon catch up with him.'

'And when we do,' said Bruce, 'I'm gonna stuff him in a sack full of bricks and chuck him in the canal.'

'Kindest thing in the long run, Bruce,' said Sheila, and they set off down the road after the rapidly disappearing ambulance.

It was even harder to drive a speeding ambulance in a pantomime wolf suit than it was to climb a tree in one, but Inspector Plonker and Sergeant Snoop managed it somehow.

'I thought vets were supposed to be kind to animals,' said Inspector Plonker. 'Those two lunatics were planning to do us in!'

'We're not animals, sir,' Sergeant Snoop reminded him, 'We're just disguised as one.'

'Anyway,' said Sergeant Snoop, 'There's that bus, right up ahead. Looks like it's heading for the Town Hall.'

Sure enough, a short distance in front of them, the bus was slowing down.

'Right, Snoop,' said Inspector Plonker, switching on the ambulance's siren, 'The Wolf is in that bus. And this time he's not going to get away.'

Meanwhile, in the police station canteen, the Chief of Police was having his tea break and watching television. He had managed to crash-land the helicopter in the station car park, where a team of mechanics was now working frantically to repair it.

The Chief had the remote control in his hand and was flicking impatiently from one channel to another when he found himself watching 'Pet Patrol'. He watched for a moment in disbelief, then leaped to his feet and rushed out of the station, yelling into his walkie-talkie as he rushed towards the helicopter.

'Calling all cars! Calling all cars!' he bellowed. 'Now hear this. A big green ambulance is driving down the high street towards the Town Hall. All units proceed to the area at once. The Wolf is in that ambulance. And this time he's not going to get away.'

Ignoring the mechanics (who were trying to give him their bill) he bounded into the helicopter and started up the engine.

With a shrill, spluttering roar, the craft rose unsteadily into the air and flew off towards the Town Hall, leaving a trail of smoke and sparks behind it.

Chapter Seven

Another Cunning Plan

As the old ladies got off the bus and hurried into the Town Hall, the Wolf deliberately lagged behind.

'Hurry up, Granny,' said Little Red Riding Hood, tugging his paw. 'All the best seats will be taken.'

'Sorry, dear,' wheezed the Wolf feebly, 'Me arthritis is playing up, not to mention me lumbago, me rheumatism and me rabies.'

As the last old lady hobbled up the steps and vanished through the big double doors, the Wolf prepared to pounce. Nobody could stop him now!

Just then, with a blare of sirens and a screech of brakes, the Big Green Ambulance skidded to a halt in front of the Town Hall and out jumped Inspector Plonker and Sergeant Snoop. Their Wolf costume hung in tatters around them. The tail was frayed, one glass eye had fallen out and the head was turned around the wrong way. But despite Sergeant Snoop's desperate efforts to open it, the zip was still stuck.

'All right, Wolf,' barked Inspector Plonker, 'You're under arrest.'

'You'll have to catch me first, copper,' growled the Wolf, and tried to grab Little Red Riding Hood. But as soon as she heard his snarling voice she knew she had been tricked once again, and she kicked him smartly on the shins.

'Where's my Granny, you rotten Wolf?' she cried. 'I bet you've locked her in the wardrobe again.'

With a curse, the Wolf ripped off his disguise and bounded up the fire escape which led to the roof of the Town Hall.

Just then more sirens blared, more brakes screeched, and suddenly there were police cars everywhere, with policemen tumbling out of them.

One of them looked at Sergeant Snoop and Inspector Plonker standing in the ragged wolf costume, and gave a great wail of misery.

'My costume,' he cried. 'Look what you've done to my beautiful costume!'

The other constables looked at him in amazement.

'What're you on about, Perkins?' asked Constable Pratt.

'The costume for the pantomime,'

sobbed Constable Perkins. 'It took me a week to sew it, and look at it now. It's ruined.'

'Wait a minute, Perkins,' said Constable Pratt. 'Are you telling me that's not the Big Bad Wolf?'

'Of course it isn't,' replied Constable Perkins, sniffing and wiping his eyes. 'It's Inspector Plonker and Sergeant Snoop. They borrowed my costume this morning and promised to look after it. Now look at it! And the show opens tonight.'

'Oh, stop blubbering, Perkins,' snapped Inspector Plonker. 'I told you before, the safety of the city is more important than show business. Now, somebody get a scissors and cut us out of this thing.'

'You insensitive beast!' cried poor constable Perkins and burst into tears.

In the end he had to be led away and given a nice cup of tea to calm his nerves.

Constable Pratt's radio crackled loudly:

'Chief to Pratt, over,' yelled a voice. 'Have you caught the Wolf yet, over?'

'Sorry, Chief,' replied Pratt. 'False alarm I'm afraid. It wasn't the Wolf after all. It was Inspector Plonker and Sergeant Snoop in a wolf suit.'

'Those blithering idiots,' bellowed the Chief furiously. 'Don't let them get away. I'm coming down to give them a piece of my mind.'

As he landed the helicopter on the Town Hall roof, the Chief of Police was in an even nastier mood than usual. That idiot Plonker had made a right mess of things again, running around in fancy dress, wasting everybody's time. The Chief would make him wish he'd never been born. Then, as he climbed out of the helicopter and hurried towards the fire escape that would bring him down to the street, the Chief stopped in amazement. For there, clambering onto the roof, were Plonker and Snoop. And they were still wearing that stupid wolf suit!

Of course, it was not Inspector Plonker and Sergeant Snoop who were climbing onto the roof. It was the Big Bad Wolf himself. However, the Chief of Police did not know this.

'Plonker!' he bellowed, rushing up to the Wolf and shaking his fist at him.

'Who are you calling a plonker?' growled the Wolf. But the Chief was too angry to listen to him.

'Idiot! Dolt! Nincompoop!' yelled the Chief, poking the wolf in the chest.

The wolf growled softly.

'It's no use pretending to growl,' scolded the Chief of Police, 'Just look at the state of you! Why, my grandmother looks more like a wolf than you do.'

The wolf snarled and showed his teeth.

'Think it's funny, do you, Plonker?' bellowed the Chief, who mistook the Wolf's bared teeth for a nervous smile. 'Going around looking like a mangy old hearthrug! Disgraceful. Take that ridiculous costume off at once.' And he reached out his hands and pulled the Wolf's ears as hard as he could.

This was the last straw. It was bad enough being called names, compared to somebody's grandmother and accused of being mangy, but the Wolf drew the line at having his ears pulled.

The Wolf pounced.

'Assaulting a superior officer, eh, Plonker?' yelled the Chief of Police. 'I'll have your badge for this!'

Grappling furiously, the Wolf and the Chief of Police fell to the ground and rolled towards the edge of the roof. For a moment they teetered on the brink, then tumbled into space. Still locked together, they dropped like a stone, bounced off the roof of the Big Green Ambulance and landed in a heap on the street, right at the feet of Inspector Plonker and Sergeant Snoop, who, with the help of Constable Perkins, had finally managed to get out of the wolf suit.

'Well done, Chief,' said Inspector Plonker. 'Looks like you've captured the Wolfgran!'

'I think they're both unconscious, sir,' said Sergeant Snoop.

'Very well then,' said the Inspector. 'Get them both into the ambulance, men.'

'Can I put the wolf suit in there too, sir?' asked Constable Perkins. 'I think I just might be able to patch it up in time for tonight's performance.'

'Oh, very well then, Perkins,' said Inspector Plonker.

So the Wolf, the Chief of Police and the tattered wolf suit were placed in the back of the Big Green Ambulance. Bruce and Sheila arrived on the scene just then, and they were ordered to drive the ambulance back to the police station. Siren blaring, the Big Green Ambulance sped away, followed by a convoy of police cars, vans and motorcycles.

But as soon as the doors of the ambulance had slammed shut, the Wolf, who was only pretending to be unconscious, sat up and looked around him. He saw the Chief of Police lying motionless on a stretcher and, in the corner, he saw the crumpled remains of the wolf suit. He looked from one to the another and then grinned a fiendish grin.

He could feel a cunning plan coming on ...

Chapter Eight

Mistaken Identity

The Big Green Ambulance sped into the police station car park and stopped outside the front door. Immediately it was surrounded by several nervous constables clutching their batons. Inspector Plonker drew his gun and nodded at Bruce and Sheila.

'Open the doors,' he ordered. They did so. Inside, the Chief of Police, his cap covering his face, still lay motionless on the stretcher. The Wolf was curled up in the corner.

Constables Pratt and Perkins jumped into the ambulance, picked up the stretcher and carried the Chief into the station. Then Inspector Plonker reached carefully inside, grabbed the Wolf by the tail and hauled him out. The Wolf fell with a thud onto the ground, then sat up and bellowed out a great roar of fury. Inspector Plonker leaped back in fright, then levelled his gun. But before he could shoot, Bruce popped a sack over the Wolf's head, pulled it down to his feet, and knotted it securely. The Wolf thrashed around in the sack, giving muffled screams of rage.

'There's no need for that kind of language,' said Inspector Plonker severely, but the Wolf just kept on roaring.

'What'll we do with him, sir?' asked Sergeant Snoop.

'I can chuck him in the canal for you if you'd like,' suggested Bruce. 'I'll just bung a few rocks in that sack and he'll sink like a stone.'

'Kindest thing in the long run,' said Sheila cheerfully.

'I thought you vets were supposed to take care of animals,' said Inspector Plonker.

'All right then, mate,' said Bruce, 'we'll shove him under a bus instead. That'll take care of him all right.'

'Oh, just go away, you sadists,' said Inspector Plonker angrily.

'Fair dinkum, mate,' said Bruce as the two vets climbed into the ambulance and started the engine. 'But just remember, sometimes you've got to be cruel to be kind.'

Inspector Plonker watched as the Big Green Ambulance sped away, then turned to Sergeant Snoop, shaking his head.

'Right, Snoop,' he said, 'let's get this prisoner into the cells.'

But just then the station door burst open and Constables Pratt and Perkins came rushing out.

'Sir, sir,' they cried. 'The Chief just tried to swallow us, sir.'

'He tried to what?' barked Inspector Plonker.

'Swallow us, sir,' said Constable Pratt. 'As soon as we got him inside he jumped off the stretcher and came after us. He had the biggest teeth I've ever seen.'

'And his eyes, sir,' said Constable Perkins, 'They were all red and glowing.'

'Er, excuse me, sir,' said Sergeant Snoop, 'but the wolf suit is gone.'

'The what?' snapped Inspector Plonker.

'The wolf suit, sir,' said Sergeant Snoop. 'We left it in the back of the ambulance with the Wolf and the Chief, sir. It's gone, sir.'

'Wolf suit? Wolf suit?' yelled Inspector Plonker. 'What do I care about the ...'

But suddenly he paused and his eyes grew wide. He looked from the station to the sack, then back again from the sack to the station.

'Perkins, Pratt,' he barked, drawing his gun again, 'Where's the Chief now?'

'Dunno, sir,' said Constable Pratt. 'Once he started trying to eat us we didn't hang about.'

At that moment an engine roared, a siren blared and a police motorcycle came speeding towards them. As they scrambled out of the way they caught a brief glimpse of the rider. He had big, furry ears, red, glowing eyes and a long, shaggy tail. And he was wearing the uniform of the Chief of Police. As the motorcycle sped off in the direction of the forest, Inspector Plonker turned and looked in horror at the struggling sack, from which muffled roars of anger could still be heard.

'We've really done it this time, Snoop,' he said.

'You certainly have, sir,' said Sergeant Snoop.

Chapter Nine

The Long Ears of the Law

It wasn't hard to work out what had happened. Not once they opened the sack and found the Chief of Police inside, dressed in the pantomime wolf suit. While the Chief lay unconscious in the Big Green Ambulance, the Wolf had put on his uniform and dressed him in the costume. Then, after the two constables had carried him into the station, he quickly made good his escape.

The Chief blamed Inspector Plonker for the whole thing, of course. He was never completely convinced that it was the Wolf, and not Plonker and Snoop, who had fought with him on the roof and then dressed him up in a disguise that caused him to be tied up in a sack and almost dumped in the canal. He immediately banned all amateur theatricals in the station, much to Constable Perkins's dismay.

However, he did find a use for some of the other pantomime costumes that had been made. He ordered Inspector Plonker and Sergeant Snoop to dress up as two of the Three Little Pigs and patrol the forest as bait, in the hope of fooling the Wolf into attacking them. Though he claimed that this was a ruse designed to capture the Wolf, Plonker and Snoop couldn't help suspecting that he was hoping they would get swallowed.

They were in less danger than they feared, however, for the Wolf had left the forest for good. At about this time, strange rumours began to circulate in the city about a mysterious, hairy policeman who patrolled the streets on a motorbike. It was said that if he caught anybody breaking the law, instead of arresting them he simply ate them on the spot.

This was enough to put a stop to the crime wave – old ladies went back to meekly paying their bus fares and bringing back their library books on time. It also made the streets safer for everybody, as criminals were afraid to do anything illegal for fear of being caught by the terrifying policeman with red, glowing eyes, long, furry ears and the biggest, sharpest teeth you've ever seen!

ALSO BY FINBAR O'CONNOR

WOLFGRAN

Granny Riding Hood has sold her house to the three little pigs and moved into the Happy-ever-after Home for Retired Fairy-tale Characters, leaving the Big Bad Wolf all on his own. What's a wolf to do? Go after her, of course!

Disguised as a little old lady, and swallowing everyone he meets, 'Wolfgran' gets closer and closer to Granny. But hot on his tail are Inspector Plonker, Sergeant Snoop and a very smart girl guide in a red hood.

Paperback €6.50/STG£4.99

Send for our full-colour catalogue

ORDER FORM

Please send me the books as marked.
I enclose cheque/postal order for € . . . .
(please add €2.50 P&P per title)
OR please charge my credit card ☐ Access/Mastercard ☐ Visa
Card Number _ _ _ _   _ _ _ _   _ _ _ _   _ _ _ _
Expiry Date __ __/__ __
Name. . . . . Tel . . . .
Address . . . .
. . . .

Please send orders to: THE O'BRIEN PRESS, 20 Victoria Road, Dublin 6, Ireland.
Tel: +353 1 4923333; Fax: + 353 1 4922777; E-mail: books@obrien.ie
Website: www.obrien.ie

Note: prices are subject to change without notice